OUTSIDE AND INSIDE YOU

BY SANDRA MARKLE

illustrated with full-color photographs

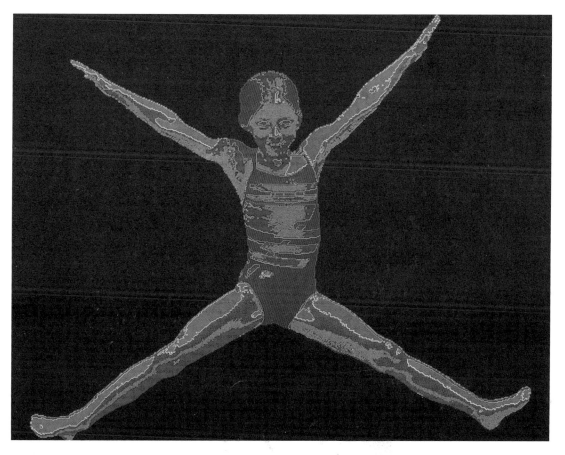

BRADBURY PRESS / NEW YORK

COLLIER MACMILLAN CANADA / TORONTO
MAXWELL MACMILLAN INTERNATIONAL PUBLISHING GROUP NEW YORK / OXFORD / SINGAPORE / SYDNEY

For Sarah and Seth Steinhoff,
who shared their wonderful curiosity

With special thanks to Dr. James E. McIntosh,
for his invaluable expertise and assistance

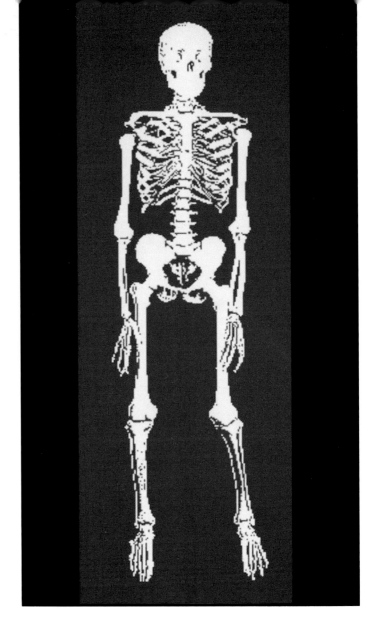

Bradbury Press
Macmillan Publishing Company
866 Third Avenue, New York, NY 10022
Collier Macmillan Canada, Inc.
1200 Eglinton Avenue East
Suite 200
Don Mills, Ontario M3C 3N1

The text of this book is set in 16 point Melior.
Book design by Christy Hale
Printed and bound in Singapore
First American Edition
10 9 8 7 6 5 4 3 2 1

Library of Congress Cataloging-in-Publication Data
Markle, Sandra.
Outside and inside you / by Sandra Markle. — 1st American ed.
*   p.   cm.*
Summary: Discusses the various parts of the body and their functions.
ISBN 0-02-762311-4
1. Body, Human—Juvenile literature. 2. Human anatomy—Juvenile
literature. [1. Body, Human. 2. Human anatomy.] I. Title.
QM27.M37   1991   612—dc20   90-37791   CIP

Look at you, at your special body. Do you ever wonder what is inside it? Or how it works? This book will let you take a peek and find out.

magnified

On your fingertip, the pattern these skin ridges form is called your fingerprint. Each of your ten fingers has a different fingerprint. Nobody in the world has identical fingerprints—not even identical twins.

Your hands are a good place to start. Hold them up and look at the backs and the palms. What you see first on the outside is skin.

Your skin is like a stretchy bodysuit just your size. It is not the same all over, though. Your skin is not even the same all over your hands.

There are hairs on the backs of your hands, for instance, but not on the palm side. That side also has ridges of skin. Do you see them?

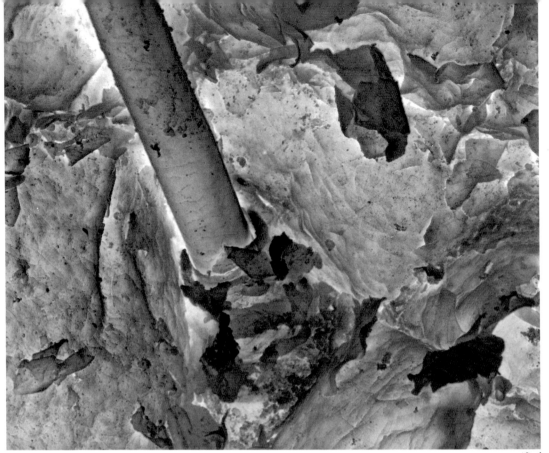

magnified

This picture is a very close look (enlarged three hundred times) at one tiny spot of skin on an arm. Do you see that polelike thing sticking out of the skin? Did you guess that it is a hair?

Now, look at the close-up picture of skin. Although your skin probably feels smooth, you can see how bumpy it really is. Do you see the curled-up flakes? Those are bits of skin. A few of these bits of skin rub off every time you brush against something. You lose even more when you wash. But don't worry. You won't ever wear a hole in your skin the way you do your clothing.

6

Your whole body, including your skin, is made of cells. Cells are like tiny building blocks. There are skin cells, muscle cells, bone cells—cells for every part of your body.

Many of the pictures in this book were taken with the help of a special tool called a microscope. Through a microscope, it's easy to see that our skin is made up of cells stacked together in layers. The cells on the outside layer are dead and form a protective coating. They get a lot of wear and flake off. But new cells underneath the old ones are constantly growing. These cells replace the ones that die.

This microscopic view of the skin has been colored to make it easier to see the layers. Notice how uneven they are. The big dips are where hairs grow. If you look closely, you will see the irregularly shaped cells which, stacked together, form the layers of skin.

color enhanced and magnified

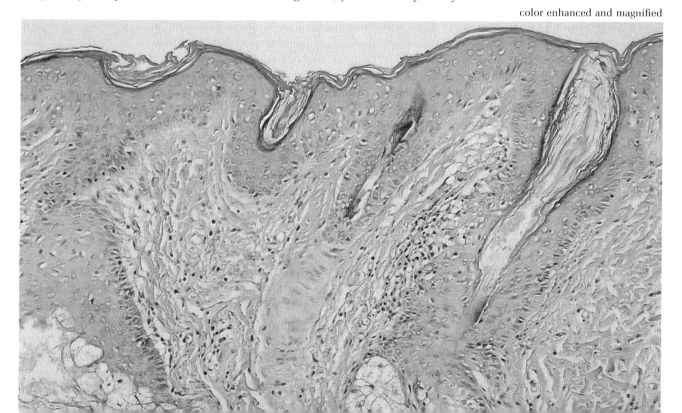

7

One of your skin's biggest jobs is to keep germs out of your body. Germs are very tiny living things. Most germs are harmless, but some are not. If germs get into a cut in your skin, they can make it become red and sore. If they get inside your body, they can make you sick.

Besides protecting you, your skin also helps your body keep a steady temperature. If you get too warm, a kind of water called sweat flows out of tiny openings, or pores, in your skin. Sweating cools you down.

color enhanced

A special heat-sensitive camera took this picture. Then a computer colored it. The hottest areas are red and yellow. The coldest areas are black.

Does it surprise you to learn that this girl's skin is not the same temperature all over? Neither is yours. While the inside of your body usually stays at a nearly constant temperature, the temperature of your skin is likely to vary. Air blowing on you or something touching your skin, like a cold floor, will affect your body's temperature at its surface.

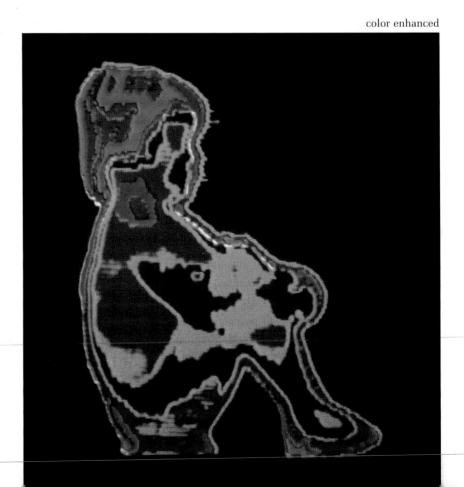

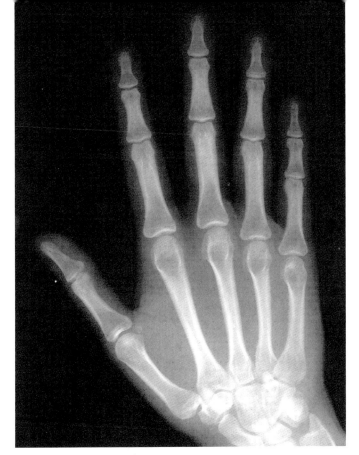

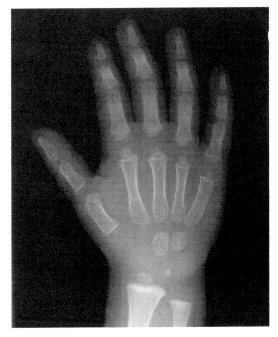

Adult's hand   *Child's hand*

Now that you've taken a close look at your body's stretchy skin, what's under it? Bones, for one thing.

A building has a strong framework to support it. You have a framework, too. Yours is a bony skeleton. Without it, you would not have any shape at all. Imagine yourself as a blob, oozing out of bed in the morning!

In special pictures called X rays, you can easily see the bones inside your body. Look at the X rays on this page. Doesn't it look like the two-year-old's hand has fewer bones than the adult's?

This is because when you are young, some of your bones are made of cartilage. Cartilage is a tough, rubbery material that does not break like hard bone. Cartilage also does not show up on an X ray. So all the bones made of cartilage in the X ray of the child's hand look like blank spaces.

By the time you are six, most of the bones in your body have become hard bone. Your hard bones are not solid like rock, though. Inside, bones look like a sponge, with lots of spaces in between hard bone. By being hard but not solid, your bones are strong enough to hold you up but also light enough so you can jump, and run, and move around easily.

Bones cannot bend. You can bend your body only at a joint, the place where two bones meet. So having lots of joints in your hands and feet lets you move them in lots of different ways. Your knees and your jaw are joints, too. What other joints can you find that let your body bend?

Some bones, like your kneecap, have another job besides holding you up: They protect parts of you. Your kneecap protects your knee joint if you get bumped or if you fall down.

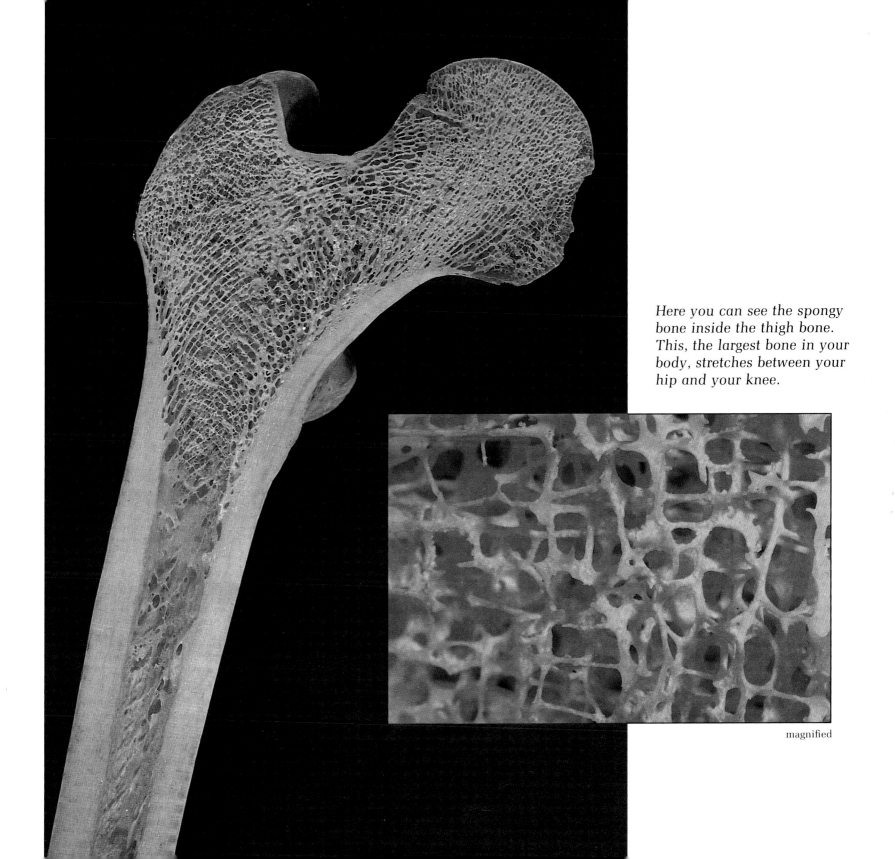

Here you can see the spongy bone inside the thigh bone. This, the largest bone in your body, stretches between your hip and your knee.

magnified

When muscles are viewed at the cell level through a microscope, you can see that they are made up of bundles of long, ropelike cells. When people exercise a lot, these cells get thicker and stronger.

Now wiggle your fingers. Make a fist. Bones support your hands, but you could not move even one finger without your muscles. Each of your hands has about thirty muscles. There are more than six hundred muscles throughout your body.

Can you lift your arm like the child in the picture? Muscles can only pull on bones, not push. So it takes two of them to move your arm up and down. The muscle on the top of the arm pulls it up, and the muscle on the bottom of your arm pulls it down again.

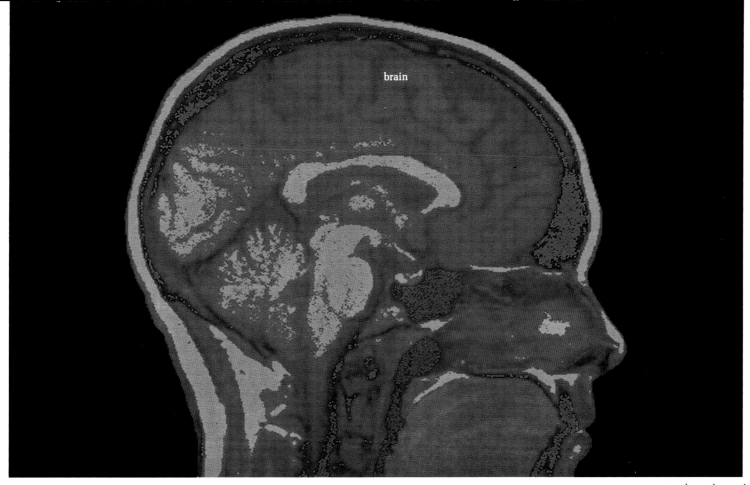

brain

color enhanced

Now here's a surprise. When you look at the pictures in this book, you don't really *see* them with your eyes. Although your eyes carry messages about what you see, it is your brain that tells you what you are seeing.

Your brain is always busy. It constantly receives messages about what is happening outside and inside your body. In a way that no one yet completely understands, your brain sorts and studies the messages it receives. Then it answers with messages of its own.

13

See the many folds that let the iris stretch and shrink to control the size of the pupil, the opening in your eye.

Look at your eyes in the mirror. See the black spot in the center of the iris, the colored part of each eye? Those spots, called pupils, are like windows that let light enter your eyes.

Do your pupils look like big black spots? Or tiny dots? You see best when the amount of light entering your eye is just right. In bright light, your pupils get smaller to block the light. In dim light, your pupils get wider to let in as much light as possible.

This is an eye in bright light.

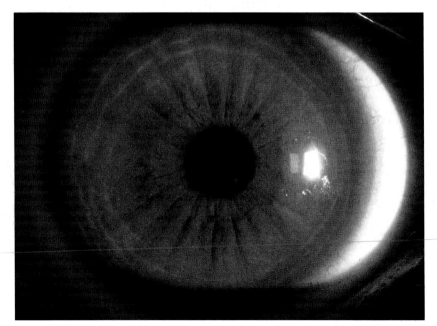

This is an eye in dim light.

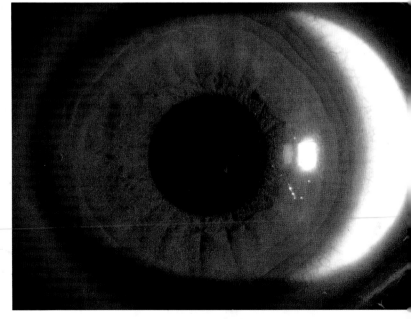

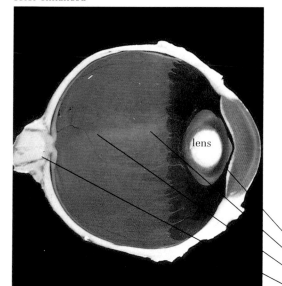

lens

iris

filled with crystal-clear jelly

retina

nerve that carries messages to the brain

This view inside an eye lets you trace the path light would follow through the eye: in the pupil, through the lens, through the crystal-clear jelly, to the light-sensitive cells on the retina.

Here you can see that two different kinds of light-sensitive cells make up the retina. The fatter, cone-shaped cells are called cones; they help you see colors. The other cells are called rods; they help you see black and white. There are many more rods than cones.

rods   cones

Once light enters your eyes, it passes through something that looks like a shiny, clear jewel. This part of the eye is called the lens. From the lens, light travels through the clear jelly inside the eye to the back of your eye, called the retina. The retina is made up of special cells. When light reaches these cells, messages are sent to your brain. As soon as your brain figures out those messages, it sends out its own signals to let you understand what you are seeing.

Of course, all this happens much faster than it takes to tell about it. In fact, it happens almost instantly.

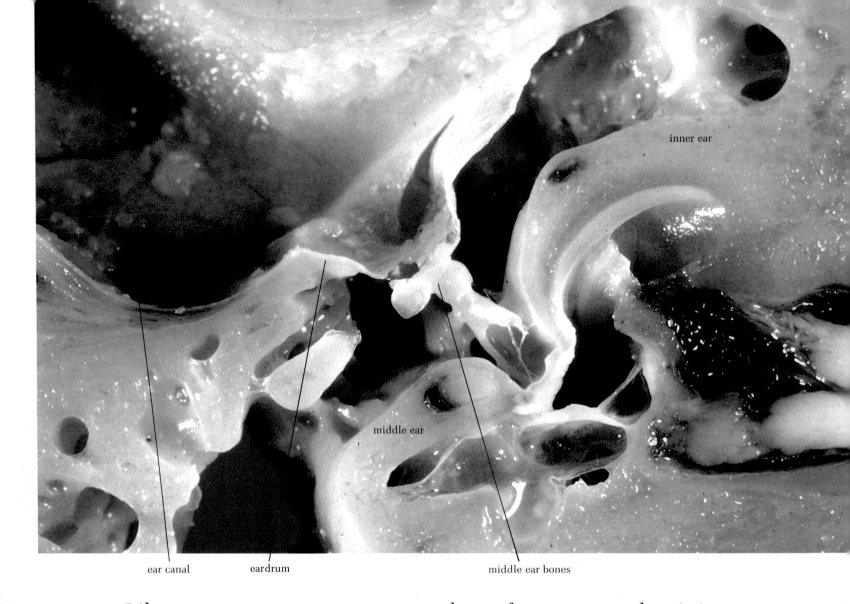

inner ear

middle ear

ear canal   eardrum   middle ear bones

Like your eyes, your ears are a pathway for messages, but it is your brain that tells you what you hear. The part of your ears that you can see is only the beginning of your ears. These flaps of skin and cartilage on the outside of your head capture sounds and direct them inside your head.

Sounds are really invisible waves of air. When sound waves first enter your ear, they pass through a short canal, bump into the eardrum, and move along the three tiny bones of the middle ear. You can follow this path in the picture on the opposite page.

Finally, the sound waves reach the inner ear, where there are special cells that send messages to your brain. Like the messages from the cells in your eyes, the messages from your ears reach your brain almost instantly. As soon as your brain puts together these messages, you hear the music, the voices, or whatever noises are around you.

Your ears are about six inches apart, so sounds often reach one ear before they reach the other. This means that your brain does not always receive messages from both of your ears at exactly the same time. When that happens, it is a clue to your brain about where a sound is coming from—above or below, from your right or your left.

Your middle ear bones got their names because of their unusual shapes. They are the tiniest bones in your body.

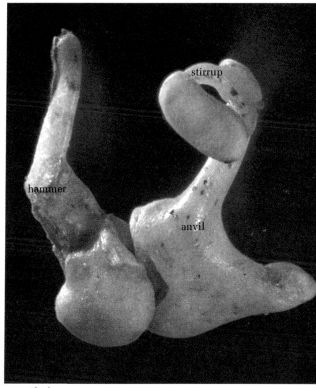

magnified

17

Now, here's a part of you that you can see without special equipment. Hold a mirror in front of your mouth. Open wide.

What a nice set of teeth! And to think you did not have any teeth at all at birth. When you were between six months and three years of age, your baby teeth appeared. There are twenty baby teeth in all. How many do you have now?

As you grow, your mouth grows, too. Between the ages of six and twelve years, your baby teeth will begin to fall out. Bigger, permanent teeth will take their place. By the time you are an adult, you will have thirty-two permanent teeth. These teeth will need to last for the rest of your life.

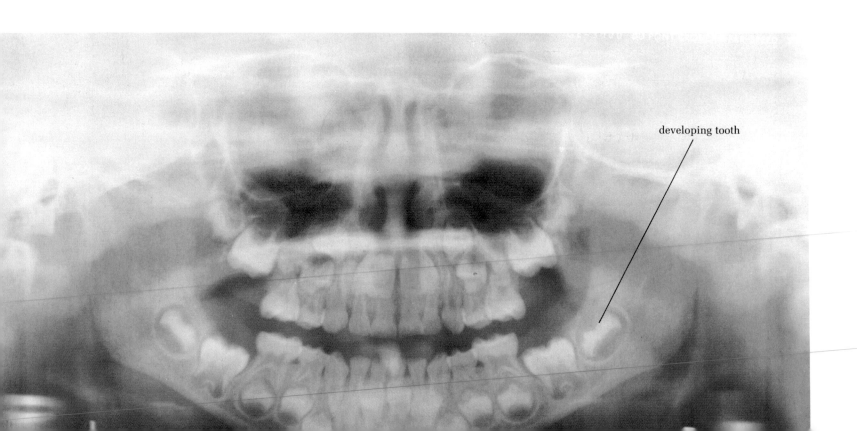

developing tooth

See what a long root this tooth has. Like tall trees, your teeth need roots. Roots hold teeth tightly in the jaw. Your teeth also have different shapes to help them perform different jobs. Look in the mirror again. You can see that your front teeth are sharp for biting. Your back teeth, though, are grooved and flattened—just right for chewing.

Now, tap one of your teeth with a fingernail. Sound hard? It is. Enamel, the coating on the outside of each tooth, is the hardest material in your body.

Germs in your mouth, however, can break through strong tooth enamel. These germs feed on bits of food that remain in your mouth after you eat. That's why it is very important to brush your teeth several times a day.

See the teeth inside the round spaces in the jawbone. These are the developing permanent teeth.

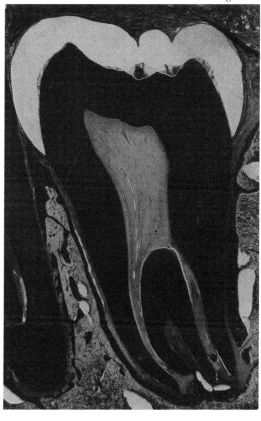

color enhanced and magnified

This is a permanent tooth ready to push up through the gum, the soft, fleshy part that surrounds your teeth. When it does, only the white, enamel-covered crown will be visible.

19

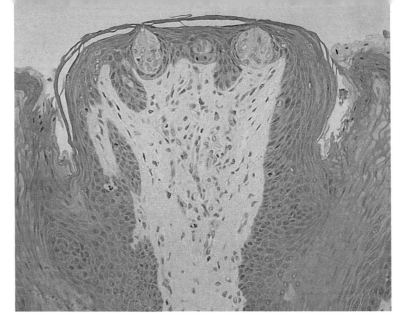

This is a close-up view of one of the many bumps on your tongue. The egg-shaped spots are taste buds.

color enhanced and magnified

Now, stick out your tongue. Wiggle it around and try curling it up. Your tongue is a very talented muscle. It helps you form sounds when you speak, whistle, and make other noises. Your tongue also helps you sense if something is cold or warm. And it helps you tell if food or drink is soft and smooth, like creamy peanut butter, or hard and rough, like dry cereal. But your tongue has another important job. It lets you taste.

Look in a mirror at the top of your tongue. See how bumpy it is? Some of those bumps are covered with egg-shaped taste buds. When things you eat or drink pass through the openings in the taste buds and reach the special cells inside, taste messages are sent to your brain. Then you are able to tell if something is sweet like candy, sour like pickles, salty like chips, or bitter like unsweetened chocolate.

But food that is dry cannot reach the special taste-sensitive cells. Try patting your tongue dry with a clean paper towel. Then place a small piece of cracker on your tongue. Notice how the cracker taste appears only when your tongue becomes wet again.

This happens because the opening in each taste bud is so small that only liquids can pass through. Saliva, the liquid in your mouth, softens and helps liquify solid food. Did you ever spill milk on a cracker and watch it fall apart? Saliva works on food the same way. Your teeth help by breaking food into small pieces which dissolve more easily.

Now, take a close look at a taste bud. See the opening where the dissolved food and drink enter.

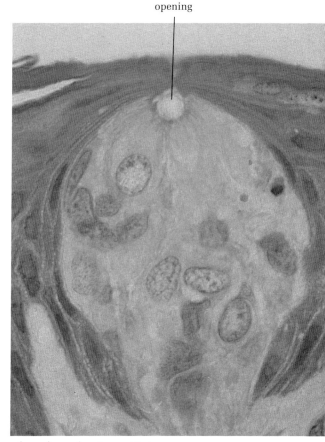

opening

color enhanced and magnified

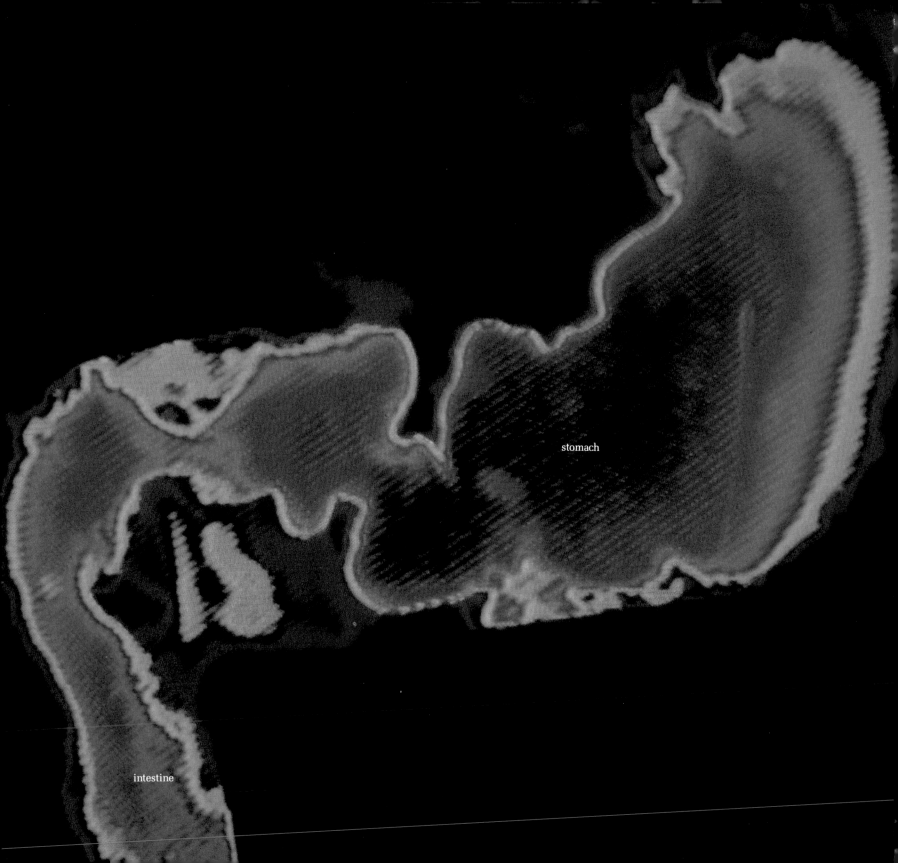

Of course, you eat food for more reasons than just its taste. Your body's cells need food for energy, so you can grow and be active. But the food you eat is not in a form that your body's cells can use. First, it needs to be broken down into tiny useful pieces called nutrients. The names of some of the nutrients which cells use are protein, vitamins, and minerals.

The breakdown begins in your mouth as soon as you start to chew and your saliva moistens the food. When you swallow, the food is moved along by muscles down a tube and into your stomach. Once in the stomach, the food is mixed with special juices from the stomach walls and squeezed by the stomach muscles until it becomes a soft paste.

The stomach has very elastic walls that stretch as it fills up with food. When this food becomes a paste, it is released into the intestine.

color enhanced and magnified

The stomach muscles squeeze about three times a minute, churning the food. Sometimes, though, these muscles squeeze when there is little or no food. Then your stomach makes loud, rumbling noises. From the stomach, the food paste is pushed into a long, winding tube called the intestine. Here, muscles squeeze the food again, mixing it with still more juices. By the time the food is broken up into its nutrient parts, the food paste has become a liquid.

color enhanced and magnified

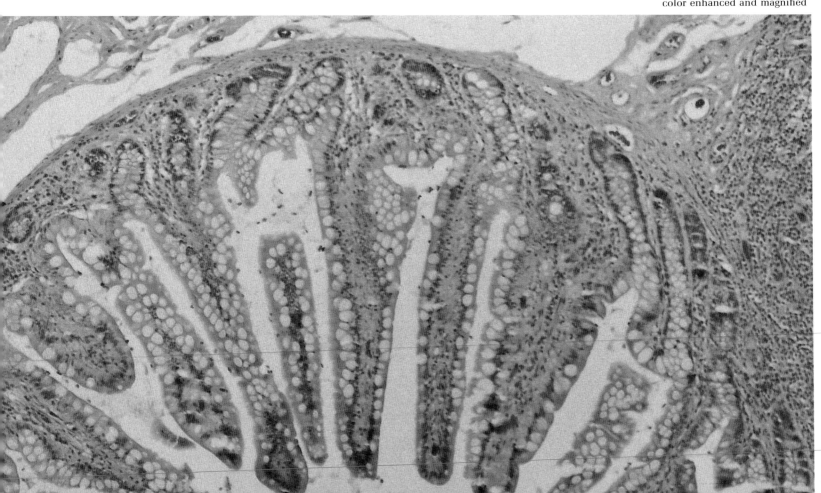

In the picture on the opposite page, you can see that the walls of the intestine are made up of many fingerlike folds. Blood flows into the middle of each of these folds. The nutrients pass through the cells of the intestine wall and enter the blood. Since blood flows throughout your body, it is able to carry the food nutrients to every cell.

Any food that is not completely broken down in the intestine becomes waste. Muscles push this waste out of your body when you have a bowel movement.

In addition to this solid waste, your body also makes liquid wastes. Some of these flow out through your skin when you sweat. If you don't bathe every day, these wastes can build up on your skin and make you smell.

Look closely at these fingerlike folds in the walls of the intestine. The white spots you see outlining each fold are the cells.

Most of your body's liquid wastes, though, are taken care of by your kidneys. Place both of your hands on your back just above your waist. Your two bean-shaped kidneys are inside. As the blood flows to your body's cells, it passes through the kidneys. Have you ever seen juice poured through a strainer, leaving fruit pulp behind? The kidneys are a kind of strainer, separating liquid wastes, called urine, from the blood.

After the clean blood leaves the kidneys, it goes on to your body's cells. The urine drips down into a holding bag called the bladder. It stays there until you go to the bathroom and let the urine out.

Muscles control the opening that lets urine leave the bladder. When you were a baby, you had to wear a diaper because you could not control these muscles.

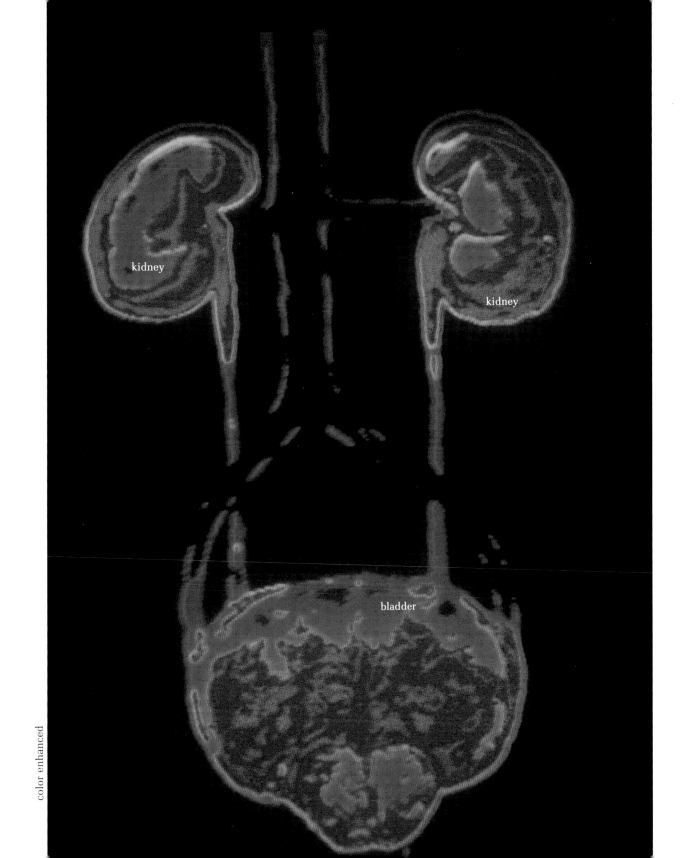

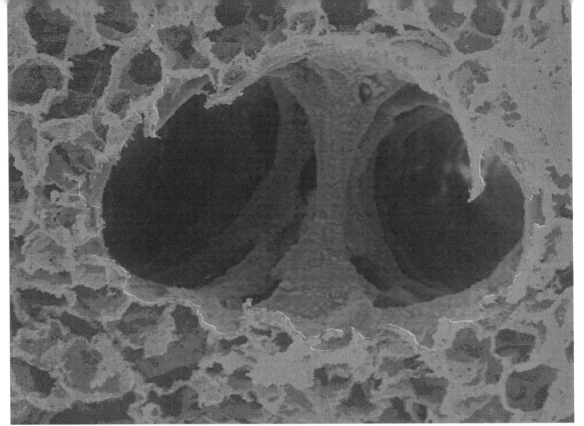

The two big holes are the ends of air tubes. The many small holes are air sacs.

color enhanced and magnified

Food is not all your body's cells need. They also need air. When you breathe, air comes in through your mouth or nose. Then it goes down a tube called the windpipe to your lungs—one on the left and one on the right side of your chest. Inside the lungs, the windpipe branches into smaller and smaller tubes. Finally, the air reaches tiny, bubblelike air sacs.

Next, oxygen, one of the gases in the air, passes into the blood surrounding each air sac and is carried to your body's cells. Your cells combine oxygen with food nutrients to produce the energy you need to be active and grow.

When you want to, you can make something special happen as air moves through your windpipe. You can make sounds.

Can you feel the bump on the front of your throat? This is your voice box, or larynx. Place your fingers gently over this spot and say "Hello." Did you feel your voice box vibrate?

When you speak or sing, you force air past two stretchy cords in your voice box. The air moves the cords, which makes sounds. Have you ever strummed rubber bands? Your vocal cords work something like that. By changing the position of your mouth and tongue, you can turn the sounds you make into words.

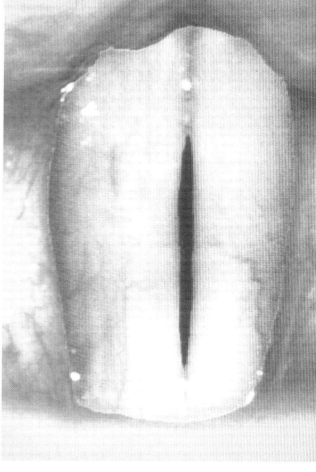

color enhanced and magnified

The bands you see on the left and right side of the opening are the vocal cords. When you make higher sounds, muscles pull on these cords, stretching them more tightly.

29

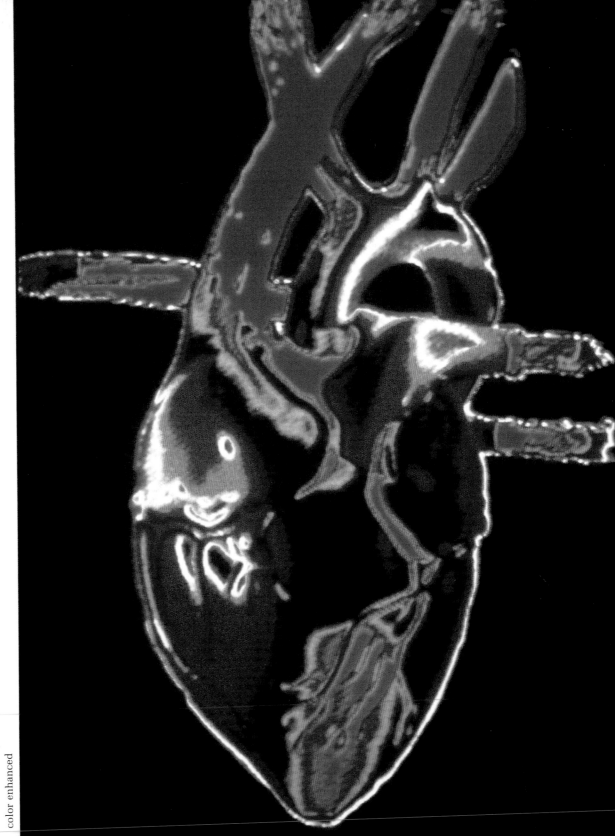

The branching tubes at the top of the heart are where the blood flows in and out of this strong muscle pump.

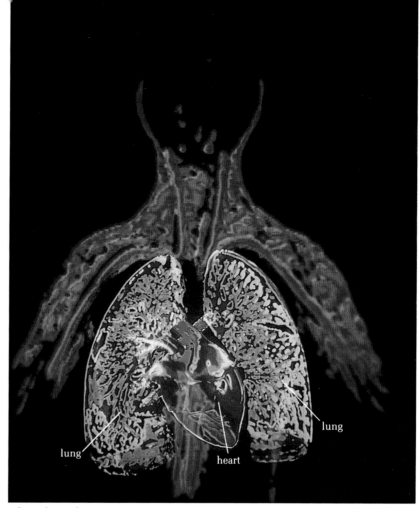

color enhanced

You have been reading about your blood moving around your body. The pump that pushes the blood is your heart. Make a fist with one hand. Your heart is about that size and shape. It lies between your lungs inside your chest.

Your heart is a muscle, but you do not have to think to make it work. Your brain keeps your heart pumping blood day and night without stopping.

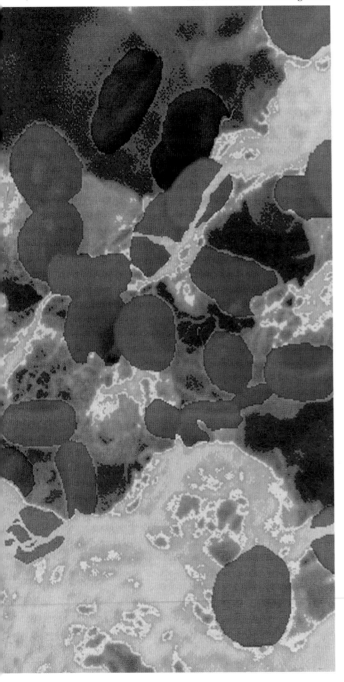

Your blood is a kind of cell soup, with different parts having different jobs. The liquid part of the blood carries the food nutrients. Special cells, the red blood cells, carry the oxygen. Other special cells, white blood cells, attack and kill any germs that get inside your body.

Blood does not just slop around inside you like water in a glass. It flows through special tubes that get smaller and smaller. Eventually, very tiny tubes carry the blood to all your body's cells. Then more tubes carry the blood back to the heart. In this way, your blood goes around and around inside your body. Look at your wrist. You can see some of these blood-carrying tubes where they are close to the surface.

The saucer-shaped red blood cells are pumped around and around your body, carrying oxygen to your cells. With all this work, each red blood cell only lasts about four months. Then, just like your skin cells, it wears out and is replaced by a new red blood cell.

Clearly, you have a wonderful body. Every part has a job to do to keep you alive. But even more important, all of your body's parts work together so you can run, jump, climb, walk, see, hear, touch, taste, smell, talk, think, and lots, lots more. You can be *you*. And that makes you a special, one-of-a-kind person from the inside out.

GLOSSARY/INDEX

Page numbers indicate text reference; boldface numbers indicate illustration.

Air sacs: Millions of tiny, bubblelike sacs at the end of the many branching airways in each lung. Here oxygen enters the blood and is carried throughout the body. 28, **28**

Bladder: A part of the body that holds urine, or liquid wastes. 26, **27**

Blood: Red liquid flowing in special tubes throughout the body that carries food and oxygen to body cells, carries wastes away from body cells, and helps fight germs. A baby's body contains about two cups of blood; an average-sized adult's body contains a little more than a gallon. 25, 26, 31, 32, **32**

Bones: The hard but lightweight parts that form the body's supporting frame. An infant has over three hundred bones, but some of these gradually fuse together to form larger single bones. By the time a child has grown to adulthood, the number of bones has decreased to 206. 9–10, **9**, **11**

Brain: Body part that receives messages about what is happening inside and outside the body and that sends messages to put the body into action. 13, **13**, 15, 17, 20, 31

Cartilage: Tough, rubbery material of which the bones of young children—generally under the age of six years—are made before they harden. Cartilage does not break like bone, and it does not show up on an X ray. 10, 16

Cells: Tiny building blocks for all body parts; muscle cells build muscles, bone cells build bones, and so on. 7, **7**, 12, 23, 26, 28, 32, **32**

Cones: These are special light-sensitive cells in the eye which respond to colors. There are actually three types of cones— those sensitive to red, green, or blue light. When the brain handles all the messages from the different cone cells, it is possible to distinguish a wide range of shades of those colors. People with faulty cones are to some degree color blind. These cells are sensitive to high-intensity light and are responsible for our best, sharpest vision. **15**

Ear canal: This body part funnels sound waves entering the ear to the eardrum. **16**, 17

Eardrum: Tightly stretched skin across the end of the ear canal which vibrates when sounds strike it. **16**, 17

Enamel: Hard coating on the outside of teeth. 19, **19**

Fingerprint: The pattern of skin ridges on fingertips which is unique for each person. Fingerprints help make it easier to grab something and hold on tight. **5**

Germs: Very tiny living things, some of which are harmful if they attack the body's cells. 8, 19

Heart: Body part that acts like a pump, constantly pushing blood throughout the body. **30**, 31, **31**, *32*

Inner ear: Sounds make ripples in this fluid-filled chamber, causing sound-sensitive cells to send messages to the brain. **16**, 17

Intestine: The long, winding tube inside the belly where food paste is mixed with juices to break it down into nutrients. These nutrients then pass into the blood and are carried through the body. If the intestine was stretched out, this tube would be a little longer than an average station wagon. 24–25, **24**

Iris: Colored part of the eye which controls how much light enters the eye. 14, **14**

Joint: Places, such as the elbow and knee, where two bones meet. Joints enable the body to bend. 10

Kidney: Body part where urine, or liquid wastes, are filtered out of the blood. 26, **26**

Larynx: Voice box where stretchy cords vibrate as air is forced out through your throat, producing sounds. Your tongue and mouth help form these sounds into words. The more air you force out, the louder the sounds. 29, **29**

Lens: Curved, clear oval structure in the eye that focuses light toward light-sensitive cells. 15, **15**

Lung: Body part where oxygen and carbon dioxide are exchanged inside tiny air sacs. 28, **31**

Middle ear: Three bones arranged in a line pass on sounds from the outer ear to the inner ear. 17, **17**

Muscles: Working in pairs, these move bones by pulling on them. There are more than six hundred muscles to move all parts of the body. 12, **12**, 20, 31

Nutrients: Chemical building blocks into which food is broken down for use by the body's cells. The five basic nutrients provided by foods are proteins, fats, carbohydrates, minerals, and vitamins. 23, 24, 32

Oxygen: A gas in the air that is breathed in and passed from the air sacs in the lungs to the blood. Then the blood carries it throughout the body. Oxygen is combined with food nutrients by the body's cells to produce energy. 28

Pores: Tiny openings in the skin through which sweat flows out onto the surface of the body. 8

Pupil: Opening in the middle of the iris that lets light enter the eye. 14, **14**

Red blood cells: Saucer-shaped blood cells that carry oxygen from the lungs to the body's cells and carbon dioxide back to the lungs. 32, **32**

Retina: Layer at the back of the eye which is made up of light-sensitive cells. When light strikes these cells, messages are sent to the brain. 15, **15**

Rods: These are light-sensitive cells that respond to forms that are black and white, sending messages to the brain. The eye contains many more rods than color-sensitive cones. These cells are sensitive to low-intensity light. **15**

Saliva: Liquid in the mouth that dissolves solid foods and begins the process of breaking food down into nutrients. 21, 23

Skeleton: Framework of bones that supports the body, gives it its shape, and provides levers for muscles to produce movement. **2**, 9, **9**

Skin: A stretchy covering that protects the body from germs and helps maintain a constant body temperature. 5–8, **5**, 6, **7**, 8

Stomach: Body part where food is mixed with special juices and squeezed until it changes into a soft paste. Sometimes the stomach squeezes when there isn't much food in it. Then it makes rumbling noises. **22**, 23

Sweat: Liquid produced by special groups of cells in the skin and poured out onto the surface to help cool off the body when it gets too warm. 8, 25

Taste buds: Special cells on the tongue that react to liquids and dissolved foods, sending messages to the brain. 20, **20**, 21, **21**

Urine: Liquid wastes. 26

Villi: Fingerlike folds in the walls of the intestine through which food nutrients pass into the blood. From there the blood carries these nutrients throughout the body. **24**

Vocal cords: Stretchy bands in the voice box that vibrate when air passes over them, creating sounds. 29, **29**

White blood cells: Blood cells that attack and get rid of germs that have entered the body. 32

Windpipe: Tube through which air moves in and out of the body. 28

ILLUSTRATION CREDITS

Front cover, pages 3, 4, and 12 (child): courtesy Susan Kuklin, photographer.

Page 1: courtesy Stephen Mann.

Page 2: courtesy Baylor Media Services Department, Baylor University Medical Center, Dallas, Texas. Colorization by Stephen Mann.

Page 5: courtesy Earth Images; Terry Domico, photographer.

Pages 6, 11, 12 (muscle cells), 19, 20, 21: courtesy Dr. James E. McIntosh and Mr. Robert D. Spears, Department of Anatomy, Baylor College of Dentistry, Dallas, Texas.

Pages 7, 17, 24, 32: courtesy Benita Ratliff, medical photographer, University of Texas Southwestern Medical Center, Dallas, Texas. Colorization page 32 by Stephen Mann.

Pages 8, 30, 31: courtesy Woodfin Camp & Associates; Howard Sochurek, photographer.

Page 9: courtesy Children's Medical Center of Dallas, Dallas, Texas.

Page 13: courtesy Dr. S. E. Harms, Baylor University Medical Center, Dallas, Texas. Colorization by Stephen Mann.

Page 14: courtesy Csaba L. Martonyi, C.O.P.R.A., W. K. Kellogg Eye Center, University of Michigan, Ann Arbor, Michigan.

Page 15: courtesy Dr. Victor Elner, W. K. Kellogg Eye Center, University of Michigan, Ann Arbor, Michigan. Photograph from Armed Forces Institute of Pathology.

Page 16: courtesy Dr. Richard A. Buckingham, Clinical Professor of Otolaryngology, University of Illinois College of Medicine, Chicago, Illinois.

Page 18: courtesy Dr. Tipton J. Asher.

Pages 22, 27: courtesy Medichrome, a Division of The Stock`Shop, Inc.; Howard Sochurek, photographer.

Page 28: courtesy Dennis Bellotto/Rolland Reynolds, University of Texas Southwestern Medical Center, Dallas, Texas. Colorization by Stephen Mann.

Page 29: courtesy Jacques Holinger Memorial Foundation. Colorization by Stephen Mann.

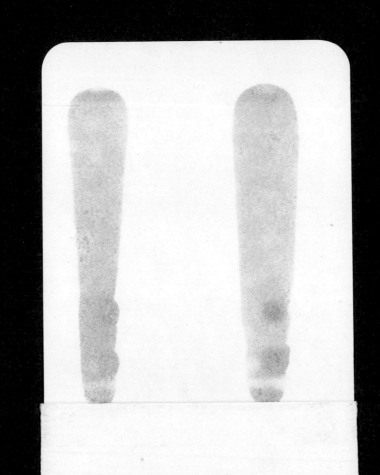